Bru

D1466530

SUJATA BHATT
BRUNIZEM

CARCANET

First published in 1988 by
Carcanet Press Limited
208-212 Corn Exchange Buildings
Manchester M4 3BQ
and
198 Sixth Avenue, New York
New York, NY 10013

Copyright © 1988 Sujata Bhatt
All rights reserved.

British Library Cataloguing in Publication Data

Bhatt, Sujata
  Brunizem.
  I. Title
  821   PR6052.H32/

ISBN 0-85635-735-9

The Publisher acknowledges financial
assistance from the Arts Council of Great Britain.

Typeset in 10pt Palatino by Bryan Williamson, Manchester
Printed in England by SRP Ltd., Exeter

In memory of Nanabhai Bhatt
and for Nachi
this book is dedicated with love

Acknowledgements

Acknowledgements are made to the editors of the following publications in which some of these poems have appeared:
Calyx, The Painted Bride Quarterly, Yellow Silk, The Iowa Journal of Literary Studies, The Reaper (USA), *Cyphers* (Ireland), *PN Review* (Great Britain), *Sjanger* (Norway).

Contents

I *The First Disciple*

Sujata: The First Disciple of Buddha | 9
The Peacock | 10
Iris | 11
Buffaloes | 13
અડેલી (Udaylee) | 15
The Doors Are Always Open | 16
શેરડી (Shérdi) | 17
Swami Anand | 18
For Nanabhai Bhatt | 20
Nachiketa | 22
Kalika | 24
For My Grandmother | 25
Muliebrity | 26
Reincarnation | 27
Lizards | 29
The First Meeting | 30
Something for Plato | 32
The Difference between Being and Becoming | 33

II *A Different History*

A Different History | 37
She Finds Her Place | 38
The Kama Sutra Retold | 39
Menu | 42
Parvati | 43
Looking Through a French Photographer's Portrayal
 of Rajasthan with Extensive Use of Orange Filters | 45
Oranges and Lemons | 47
The Women of Leh are such – | 48
Paper and Glass | 49
Another Act for the Lübecker Totentanz | 50
What Is Worth Knowing? | 51
Another Day in Iowa City | 53
Living with Trains | 54

Baltimore   57
The Woodcut   58
The Puppets   59
Pink Shrimps and Guesses   60
Looking Over What I Have Done   61
Hey,   62
Search for My Tongue   63

III *Eurydice Speaks*
Marie Curie to Her Husband   73
Clara Westhoff to Rainer Maria Rilke   74
For Paula Modersohn-Becker   76
The Garlic of Truth   77
Wanting Agni   79
Eurydice Speaks   82
Mein lieber Schwan   83
Written After Hearing About the Soviet Invasion
     of Afghanistan   84
3 November 1984   86
You Walk into This Room and   87
Mappelmus   88
The Undertow   89
At the Marketplace   91
Metamorphoses II: A Dream   92
Saturday Night on Keswick Road   95
The Writer   96
Sad Songs with Henna Leaves   97
Tail   99
Go to Ahmedabad   100
To My Muse   103
Brunizem   105
Well, Well, Well,   106

I

The First Disciple

Sujata: The First Disciple of Buddha

One morning, a tall lean man
stumbled towards me.
His large eyes: half closed
as if he were seasick;
his thick black hair full of dead leaves and bumble-bees
grew wild as weeds and fell way below his hips.
His beard swayed gently as an elephant's trunk.
"I'm hungry," he muttered.
I took him home, fed him fresh yogurt and bread.
Then, I bathed him, shaved his face clean and smooth,
coconut oiled his skin soft again.
It took four hours
to wash and comb his long hair,
which he refused to cut.
For four hours he bent his head this way and that
while I ploughed through his hair
with coconut oil on my fingers.
"And *how* did you get this way?" I asked.
"I haven't slept for years," he said.
"I've been thinking, just thinking.
I couldn't sleep or eat
until I had finished thinking."
After the last knot
had been pulled out of his hair, he slept,
still holding on to my sore fingers.
The next morning, before the sun rose,
before my father could stop me,
he led me to the wide-trunked, thick-leafed bodhi tree
to the shady spot where he had sat for years
and asked me to listen.

The Peacock

His loud sharp call
seems to come from nowhere.
Then, a flash of turquoise
    in the pipal tree.
The slender neck arched away from you
    as he descends,
and as he darts away, a glimpse
    of the very end of his tail.

I was told
that you have to sit in the veranda
    and read a book,
preferably one of your favourites
    with great concentration.
The moment you begin to live
inside the book
a blue shadow will fall over you.
The wind will change direction,
the steady hum of bees
in the bushes nearby
will stop.
The cat will awaken and stretch.
Something has broken your attention;
and if you look up in time
you might see the peacock
turning away as he gathers in his tail
to shut those dark glowing eyes,
violet fringed with golden amber.
It is the tail that has to blink
for eyes that are always open.

Iris

Her hand sweeps over the rough grained paper,
then, with a wet sponge, again.
A drop of black is washed grey,
cloudy as warm breath fogging cool glass.
She feels she must make the best of it,
she must get the colour of the stone wall,
of the mist settling around twisted birch trees.
Her eye doesn't miss the rabbit crouched,
a tuft of fog in the tall grass.
Nothing to stop the grey sky from merging into stones,
or the stone walls from trailing off into sky.
But closer, a single iris stands fully opened:
dark wrinkled petals, rain-moist,
the tall slender stalk sways, her hand follows.
Today, even the green is tinged with grey,
the stone's shadow lies heavy over the curling petals
but there's time enough, she'll wait,
study the lopsided shape.
The outer green sepals once enclosing the bud
lie shrivelled: empty shells spiralling
right beneath the petals.
As she stares the sun comes out.
And the largest petal flushes
deep deep violet.
A violet so intense it's almost black.
The others tremble indigo, reveal
paler blue undersides.
Thin red veins running into yellow orange rills,
yellow flows down the green stem.
Her hand moves swiftly from palette to paper,
paper to palette, the delicate brush
swoops down, sweeps up,
moves the way a bird builds its nest.
An instant and the sun is gone.
Grey-ash-soft-shadows fall again.
But she can close her eyes and see

11

red-orange veins, the yellow
swept with green throbbing towards blue,
and deep inside she feels
indigo pulsing to violet.

Buffaloes

The young widow
thinks she should have burned on
her husband's funeral pyre.
She could not, for her mother-in-law
insisted she raise the only son
of her only son.
The young widow sits outside
in the garden overlooking a large pond.
Out of the way, still untouchable, she suckles
her three-week-old son
and thinks she could live
for those hungry lips; live to let him grow
bigger than herself. Her dreams lie
lazily swishing their tails
in her mind like buffaloes
dozing, some with only nostrils showing
in a muddy pond.

Tails switch
to keep fat flies away,
and horns, as long as a man's hand, or longer
keep the boys, and their pranks away.
It is to the old farmer's tallest son
they give their warm yellowish milk.
He alone approaches: dark-skinned and naked
except for a white turban, a white loincloth.
He joins them in the pond,
greets each one with love:
"my beauty", "my pet" –
slaps water on their broad flanks
splashes more water on their dusty backs.
Ears get scratched, necks rubbed,
drowsy faces are splashed awake.
Now he prods them out of the mud
out of the water, begging loudly
"Come my beauty, come my pet, let us go!"
And the pond shrinks back
as the wide black buffaloes rise.

The young widow
walks from tree to tree,
newly opened leaves brush damp sweet smells
across her face. The infant's mouth sleeps
against her breast. Dreams stuck
inside her chest twitch
as she watches the buffaloes pass
too close to her house, up the steep road
to the dairy. The loud loving voice
of the farmer's son holds them steady
without the bite of any stick or whip.

અડેલી *(Udaylee)**

Only paper and wood are safe
from a menstruating woman's touch.
So they built this room
for us, next to the cowshed.
Here, we're permitted to write
letters, to read, and it gives a chance
for our kitchen-scarred fingers to heal.

Tonight, I can't leave the stars alone.
And when I can't sleep, I pace
in this small room, I pace
from my narrow rope-bed to the bookshelf
filled with dusty newspapers
held down with glossy brown cowries and a conch.
When I can't sleep, I hold
the conch shell to my ear
just to hear my blood rushing,
a song throbbing,
a slow drumming within my head, my hips.
This aching is my blood flowing against,
rushing against something –
knotted clumps of my blood,
so I remember fistfuls of torn seaweed
      rising with the foam,
rising. Then falling, falling up on the sand
strewn over newly laid turtle eggs.

*   અડેલી   (Udaylee): untouchable when one is menstruating

15

The Doors Are Always Open

Everywhere you turn there are goats,
some black and lumpy.
Others, with oily mushroom-soft hair,
sticky yellow in Muslim sand
shaded by the mosque.
Next door
there's a kerosene smeared kitchen.
We share a window
with the woman who lives with goats.
Now she unwraps some cheese
now she beats and kneads
a little boy   and screams
"Idiot! Don't you tease that pregnant goat again!"
I look away: outside
the rooster runs away
from his dangling sliced head
while the pregnant goat lies with mourning hens.
Her bleating consolations
make the children spill
cheesy milk and run outside.
Wet soccer ball bubbles roll out
from a hole beneath the lifted tail.
The goat licks her kids free,
pushing, pushing
until they all wobble about.
We've counted five.
Hopping up and down, we push each other
until we see
the goat pushing her kids
to stand up, until
mothers call us back
                    to thick milk.

શેરડી   *(Shérdi)**

The way I learned
to eat sugar cane in Sanosra:
I use my teeth
to tear the outer hard *chaal*
then, bite off strips
of the white fibrous heart –
suck hard with my teeth, press down
and the juice spills out.

January mornings
the farmer cuts tender green sugar-cane
and brings it to our door.
Afternoons, when the elders are asleep
we sneak outside carrying the long smooth stalks.
The sun warms us, the dogs yawn,
our teeth grow strong
our jaws are numb;
for hours we suck out the *russ*, the juice
                                    sticky all over our hand

So tonight
when you tell me to use my teeth,
to suck hard, harder,
then, I smell sugar cane grass
                    in your hair
and imagine you'd like to be
shérdi   shérdi   out in the fields
            the stalks sway
                    opening a path before us

---

*   શેરડી   (Shérdi): sugar cane

17

Swami Anand

In Kosbad during the monsoons
there are so many shades of green
your mind forgets other colours.

At that time
I am seventeen, and have just started
to wear a sari every day.
Swami Anand is eighty-nine
              and almost blind.
His thick glasses don't seem to work,
they only magnify his cloudy eyes.
Mornings he summons me
        from the kitchen
and I read to him until lunch time.

One day he tells me
"you can read your poems now"
I read a few, he is silent.
Thinking he's asleep, I stop.
But he says, "continue".
I begin a long one
in which the Himalayas rise
              as a metaphor.
Suddenly I am ashamed
to have used the Himalayas like this,
ashamed to speak of my imaginary mountains
to a man who walked through
        the ice and snow of Gangotri
              barefoot
a man who lived close to Kangchenjanga
        and Everest clad only in summer cotton.
I pause to apologize
but he says "just continue".

Later, climbing through
        the slippery green hills of Kosbad,
Swami Anand does not need to lean
on my shoulder or his umbrella.
I prod him for suggestions,
ways to improve my poems.
He is silent a long while,
then, he says
        "there is nothing I can tell you
                except continue."

For Nanabhai Bhatt

In this dream my grandfather
comes to comfort me.
He stands apart
silent
and in his face I see
the patience of his trees
on hot typhoid days
that promise no rain.

His eyes
the colour of a crow's feather in children's mud,
yet filled with sharp mountain-top light.

I'm sure this was the face the true bald man,
Gandhiji saw when he confessed
about the Harijan girl, the six-year-old
he adopted and tried to educate.
I'm sure these were the eyes the true hermaphrodite,
Gandhiji saw while he explained
how this girl cared too much for clothes,
how one day she went and had her hair bobbed,
the latest fashion, she said.
It was too much.
She had to be set straight,
the sooner the better.
So he had her head shaved
to teach her
not to look in mirrors so often.
At this point Gandhiji turned
towards my grandfather and allowed, so softly:
"But she cried.
I couldn't stop her crying.
She didn't touch dinner.
She cried all night.
I brought her to my room,
tucked her in my bed, sang her *bhajans*,
but she still cried.
I stayed awake beside her.

So this morning I can't think clearly,
I can't discuss our plans
for building schools in villages."
And my grandfather
looked at him with the same face
he shows in my dream.

Nachiketa

for my brother

The bird was fat-brown limp feathers,
half-deflated limp dull brown
and seemed to be sweating
all the time. And Nachiketa carried
it around in a floppy straw hat
fluttering orange ribbons with his mother's sunny
rice-paddy green silk scarf inside,
nestling the sticky claws
and half-coma-shut eyes.
Yes, Nachiketa, five years old and frowning,
held the straw hat nest all day, walked
through the house from balcony
to balcony, upstairs and down
from terrace to garden and back again.

Did you know that long ago Nachiketa visited
great Yamaraj?* Yes, long ago
Nachiketa travelled through jaundiced grass
past choleraed cows, past black-lunged horses
standing beneath leprosied trees.
And great Yamaraj was not home.
So Nachiketa waited. Hungry. Nachiketa
sat on the dark doorstep in sunless heat.
Nachiketa waited for three days.
Hungry.

Then, Yama arrived delighted
with Nachiketa's patience,
and Yama arrived ashamed
to have been an absent host.
And so of course there were three boons
to be granted, three wishes to be had.
Take your three wishes and please leave,
this is no place for curious children,
no place for the alive and Karma unfulfilled.
But Nachiketa stood still.
Not wanting but asking.

Not wanting a thing but asking all.
And great Yamaraj relented
saying, oh all right, all right I'll tell you.

The first time Nachiketa returned
from the house of Yama, his skin was yellow
and he slept in an incubator for a month.
The second time Nachiketa returned
from the house of Yama,
he found the bird wheezing and croaking
by the dirt road.
The eighth time Nachiketa visited the house of Yama
I followed, cursing every god, every being
every spirit that could possibly exist.
I followed cursing until Nachiketa returned
safe again.

Each time Yamaraj gives Nachiketa
a different fact, fresh secrets...
But what did he feed Nachiketa?
And what did Nachiketa drink
with great Yamaraj?
Sometimes I dream Yama's hand
brushing against Nachi's shirt
when he reached for a plate of something.

I walk about bored, I walk about
wishing I had such secrets –
While Nachiketa sits in the garden
by the sunflowers
with the straw hat in his lap.
He sings all afternoon
while the bird wheezes back
and he continues singing
even when the bird does not move.

* Yamaraj: the god of death

Kalika

In the morning, while Kalika combs
her seven-year-old daughter's glossy tangled hair,
she looks at her face in the mirror;
red-eyed, worn out,
she feels she has grown into a mangy stranger overnight.
Her daughter's face: wide open eyes
so much more like her mother's
who died last night
in a diabetic coma.

As Kalika parts the hair in the centre,
a straight line curving down
the back of her daughter's head;
she remembers, five years ago
blisters on the back of her mother's head
grew and grew, never healing,
her mother's scalp cracked and bleeding
until the doctor shaved off
the waist-length thick grey hair
and tightly bandaged the head.

As Kalika watches her daughter open the door
the sun falls on the bright red ribbons
flowering at the ends of the freshly made braids,
and there is her mother in a red sari,
walking towards the sound of temple bells.
Green herbs, white jasmine in her hands,
tiny red blossoms woven in her coiling hair.

Later, tearing out sticky cobwebs
from corners in the high ceiling,
while jabbing at fleeing spiders with a long-handled broom,
Kalika winces, glances out the window
and sees her daughter on the lawn
struggling with her doll's matted hair.

For My Grandmother

Aaji, there was an eleven-year-old girl
who sat on our doorstep
during the feast
of your mourning.
She would not cry or eat
              sleep or speak.
Now they make dolls
who do all of those things.

              And I could not explain
              about my taut
              four hours of sleep
              in the closet, on the floor
              with your softly dying clothes.

Muliebrity

I have thought so much about the girl
who gathered cow-dung in a wide, round basket
along the main road passing by our house
and the Radhavallabh temple in Maninagar.
I have thought so much about the way she
moved her hands and her waist
and the smell of cow-dung and road-dust and wet canna lilies,
the smell of monkey breath and freshly washed clothes
and the dust from crows' wings which smells different –
and again the smell of cow-dung as the girl scoops
it up, all these smells surrounding me separately
and simultaneously – I have thought so much
but have been unwilling to use her for a metaphor,
for a nice image – but most of all unwilling
to forget her or to explain to anyone the greatness
and the power glistening through her cheekbones
each time she found a particularly promising
mound of dung –

Reincarnation

The wise old men
    of India say
there are certain rules.
For example, if you loved
your dog too much,
in your next life you'll be a dog,
yet full of human memories.
And if the King's favourite daughter
loved the low-caste palace gardener
who drowned while crossing the river
in a small boat during the great floods,
they'll be reborn, giving a second chance.
The wise old men of India say
one often dreams
of the life one led before.

There's a lion sprawled out
beside his cubs.
His thick mane tangled with dry grass,
his head droops: dusty stooping dahlia.
Then with a shudder,
      a sudden shake of his head
he groans and growls
at four whimpering cubs.
(He'd let them climb
all over his back
if only he weren't so hungry.)
The lioness is already far away
hunting in the deepest part of the valley:
a tall dark forest.
Red-flowered vines,
gold-flecked snakes encircling every tree.
Tall ferns,
fringes of maidenhair edging broad leaves.
But now the lioness steps out
into a vast clearing.
She lifts her head towards the east, the west:
sniffing, sniffing. Her eyes stare hard,

urgent, she walks as if her raw swollen teats,
pink and not quite dry, prickle and itch
and goad her on.
She's lean enough, afraid
her cubs might die.
Now there's clear water flowing rapidly,
rippling over rocks, the lioness stops, drinks,
her quick long tongue licks, laps up the water.
Now the lioness is wading through, swimming,
her long golden tail streams through rushing waves;
torn, bruised paws splashing.
A quiet breeze
          as if the earth were barely breathing.
Fallen leaves, still green,
and tangled vines swirl in the water,
          the lioness circling.
Nearby monkeys, squirrels,
even birds remain hidden, silence.
A dead bull elephant rots:
          bullet-pocked, tuskless.

You hold me, rock me,
pull me out of my dream,
(or did I dream you?)
The fur lingers on your skin,
your body has not forgotten
how to move like a cat.
Look, the sun spills golden over the walls,
you grow tawnier with the dawn.
Shivering haunches relax,
the slow licking begins
gently over the bruises.

Lizards

It's a loud darkness tonight,
filled with the hard noise
of breath after angry breath.
I stare at the blank wall,
dingy and lizard-green –
it needs to be repainted
some other colour, you say, off-white, yellow,
anything but this green.

I learned to stare at the walls
in Maninagar in the summertime
when the lizards come inside.
Nights they lingered on the walls,
followed thick insects across the ceiling
while I squirmed in bed
entwined with shadows of leaves and lizards.
Their black eyes: round mustard seeds glistened.
And I stared at them, felt them secretly snickering.
I stared, trying not to blink,
afraid they would plop in bed with me.

Tonight
when you look at me
with your hard unblinking eyes,
the noise of flies and mosquitoes
gnaws through my ears.
That's when my dreams become lizards:
delicate feet walk up my neck
over my forehead, through my hair, I can feel
their long slender tails trail across my skin
almost like those moist tendrils the wind blew
across my face the other day.
My dreams come and touch us,
like soft paintbrushes thick with colour,
like fingers wet with paint.
And we can still finger paint,
why not?
Let's finger paint with all your tongues and lips
and sperm across our hips.

29

The First Meeting

When I run past the uncounted trees,
groves of mango, eucalyptus –
how the grass slips beneath my feet,
how the wind circles up my legs,
    (invisible snake I can't escape)
how the kingfisher-blue sky grows
sunnier each second as I run
    up the hill almost blinded,
        run down the other side, my tongue dry,
to the lake where the sky is trapped, tamed blue.
But closer, it is clear water. As I drink
green snakes swim up to the surface,
I recoil amazed, run back faster, faster.

When I get home
he's there: King Cobra
tightly curled up in a corner.
He looks tired.
    "Come inside, close the door,
    don't run away," he seems to smile.
    "I live in your garden.
    I chose it because of the huge purple-golden dahlias.
    I've never seen such tall stalks,
    such plump flowers, and the mice!"
    "What do you want?" I ask afraid
his sunken hood will expand.
    "Oh you needn't worry, you needn't worship me
as all the rest do. Please don't change.
Everywhere I go people pester me
with their prayers,
their hundred bowls of milk a day.
There's only so much milk I can drink.
I won't be caught
and have my teeth pulled out.
I won't be stuffed in a basket
and commanded to rise, wave after wave,
to ripple around the straw rim.
As if their baskets could contain me,

as if their bulging pipes could move me.
        Oh I am sooo tired..." he sighs.
"What do you want?" I ask.
"I want to live in your garden,
to visit you, especially those nights you sing,
let me join you.
And once in a while, let me lie around your neck
and share a bowl of milk..."

Something for Plato

He holds out his lips,
this wreck of a rhinoceros:
dried-up gravel skin, limping with a crooked spine –
but who knows, maybe he's happy
kept like this in the Delhi zoo. Here he walks
like a fat man in a crisp red sports jacket
who doesn't think of himself as fat – he's so pleased
with the virile cut of his new sports jacket...

Flabby cracked lips
shudder open, showing us a sharp triangular
smiling tongue. He keeps lifting up
those thick scabby rough lips, wobbling
with such a tender gesture,
an emotion so strong
the lines around his neck are suddenly delicate –
so graceful – he could be a young flamingo, a weeping willow,
leaving no doubt
that he wants to be caressed. There's plenty
of grass around him
but he won't have it, he wants
to be hand-fed, wants his forehead stroked.
He'll put up with having his horn pulled at,
pretend his head can be jerked around
by the scrawny schoolboys – as long as they feed him,
the tips of their fingers arousing and soothing his mouth.

The Difference Between Being and Becoming

So where *does* the body house the soul?
Locked in the attic,
wings whirring against glass?
                No.
These doors and windows are always open.

As children we lived outside.
Beyond the house
the well was cool black stones
inside rings of wet black soil.
And inside that, a clear round mirror?
But steps lead down
to water funny as jambu juice.
We reach in up to our elbows;
I drink so the water runs down my shirt.

Then, we'd run beyond the well
to a neem tree, Durga's tree.
Sullen narrow leaves
scatter soft yellow berries,
sticky limbollis everywhere.
We gather some in our pockets,
suck on the hard seeds.
The pulp tastes almost like sugar cane
except for the slight bitterness
each time I swallow.

Then, we'd roam beyond the neem tree,
close to the tall hedge
where a huge hibiscus sways
                thrumming
throbbing with the hummingbird inside.

II

A Different History

A Different History

Great Pan is not dead;
he simply emigrated
       to India.
Here, the gods roam freely,
disguised as snakes or monkeys;
every tree is sacred
and it is a sin
to be rude to a book.
It is a sin to shove a book aside
       with your foot,
a sin to slam books down
       hard on a table,
a sin to toss one carelessly
       across a room.
You must learn how to turn the pages gently
without disturbing Sarasvati,*
without offending the tree
from whose wood the paper was made.

2

Which language
has not been the oppressor's tongue?
Which language
truly meant to murder someone?
And how does it happen
that after the torture,
after the soul has been cropped
with a long scythe swooping out
of the conqueror's face –
the unborn grandchildren
grow to love that strange language.

* Sarasvati: the goddess of knowledge. She presides over all the Fine Arts and is worshipped in libraries.

She Finds Her Place

Oh but he wanted a wife,
Shileyko did –
a wife, not a poet,
so he burnt Anna's poems
    in the samovar.

And I yelled at you
when all you did
was spill some tea
(quite accidentally) over my poems.

Now outside in the snow
I'm looking for the tallest pine tree,
the one whose sly wisdom I need.
Now outside in the snow
I'm thinking of Anna. Over there
it's always dark. The sky
if not grey, is black.
The snow thigh high
slowly grows waist deep.
But the tall woman, her dark shawl
pulled taut, walks on anyway.
The tall woman walks alone,
deeper into the woods
among a crowd of trees
she finds her place
and looks at the moon
as if it were her little sister
finally come home.

The Kama Sutra Retold

Then Roman Svirsky said,
"it is illegal in Russia to write
                about sex
so it is important
for Vasily Aksyonov
to write about it –"

You laugh,
but I want to know
how would we break the long silence
if we had the same rules?

It's not enough to say
                she kissed his balls,
            licked his cock long
                how her tongue could not stop.

For he thinks of the first day:
she turns her head away
as she takes off her T-shirt
blue jeans, underwear, bra.
She doesn't even look at him
until she's in the lake,
the clear water up to her neck
yet unable to hide her skin.

They swim out
        to the islands
but he doesn't remember swimming;
just brushing against her leg
                once, then diving down
beneath her thighs   staying underwater
    long enough for a good look,
coming up for air   and watching
   her black hair streaming back straight,
then watching her
        step over
            the stones, out of the water.

39

She doesn't know what to say.
He wishes they were swans,
      Yeats's swans
  would not need to speak
but could always glide across
    other worlds;
magical, yet rustling with real reeds.

The sun in her eyes
so they move closer to the pine trees.
When he touches her nipples
he doesn't know
who is more surprised
(years later he remembers that look,
 the way her eyes open wider).
He's surprised
she wants him
to kiss her nipples again and again
because she's only 17 he's surprised
her breasts are so full.
She's surprised
     it feels so good
because he's only 17 she's surprised
he can be so gentle
    yet so hard inside her,
the way pine needles
    can soften the ground.
Where does the ground end
  and she begin?
She must have swallowed the sky
  the lake, and all the woods
         veined with amber brown pathways;

for now great white wings
are swooping through
her thighs, beating stronger
  up her chest,
the beak stroking her spine
feathers tingling her skin,

the blood inside
            her groin swells

while wings are rushing to get out,
                    rushing.

Menu

Wet, black, invisible-shadow-sheer
from mulberry flavoured silk –

And he wanted his oysters served
on these black stockings with open violets –

And he wanted dry dry wine
with oysters on this invisible silk –

While outside, the hearts of Pacific waves
that never return to the sea –

And as he drinks, Pacific froth lingers on
salty on his cheeks and lips –

While the bridge breathes red and gold shadow silk
strong and steady silk: red, gold, red –

And as he slips oysters in his mouth
his lips turn gold: breathe red silk –

While outside, Pacific waves slap up, splashing
legs, thighs, making wet these black stockings –

And he turns to the dry sheer dry wine,
a soft sip after each silky oyster –

Parvati

If this myth is alive
for me then why isn't it for you?
How does a myth stay alive?
How many people does one need in order
to keep a myth alive?

Do you know what it feels like
to pick green tea-leaves that grow
on the other side of the path across from the guava trees –
to pick green tea-leaves
moments before the water boils?

I don't know why I turn to Parvati, daughter
of the Himalayas – but I do.
"Parvati, oh Parvati
where is the mountain today, where did you
take it away?
Parvati
oh Parvati, hide the tea-leaves
while they're still growing –
don't let them come near Darjeeling.

Parvati
why did you let Twinings take everything?

Parvati
I must confess
I like Twinings the best.

Do you wash your hair everyday?
Do you have enough *shikakai*?"

In the first story she was
taking a bath, washing her hair,
becoming drowsy in the soft water,
she was slow, she dawdled in order to regain
all her energy
all her shakti-fragrant self
            for Shiva.

Those whose blood flows to the rhythm of om
whose souls resound om, om,
clear om, underwater om,
om spontaneously
without ever meaning to say it –
That om caught Parvati and kept her
alive, and keeps her always bathing
always braiding her hair.

I must have breathed om, however accidentally,
because Parvati stops me.
We argue. Why should I fight with her?
But I do.
Why can't she even protect the tea leaves?

Heathen.
Pagan. Hindu.
What does it mean, what is a pagan?
Someone who worships fire?
Someone who asks Parvati to account for
the Industrial Revolution.

Looking Through a French Photographer's Portrayal of Rajasthan with Extensive Use of Orange Filters

What has happened over here?
Has the day turned orange?
Or am I looking at these men
                    through flames?
Such loud crackling colours of wood,
as if fifty warriors were burning
                    on their funeral pyres,
as if fifty widows were running in
                    to join the saffron fire.

I am here   on one side
and the turbanned men are standing
                    on the other side.
They stand stiff
            jaws tight
unaccustomed to watching someone take aim
                            at their heads.
Somehow they don't notice the fire
    but look calmly beyond
                    the flames
to the horizon.
And as I focus on their eyes
I too begin to see the cacti sprouting
                    in miles and miles of sand.
    As I follow their eyes
I find footprints of men and camels
            leading to the sky.

Next   the women
            tall and straight-backed
odhanis draped
            over their heads
the young girls
with large brass pitchers
balanced on their heads
are on their way home
                    from the well.

45

Mirrors embroidered
   on peacock-green skirts
are swinging around their ankles.
Hurry, the women are moving briskly,
their faces are turned away
and the odhanis
   hide their profiles.
There is also yellow fog
   or is it smoke?
Orange mist hissing out of the bushes
   so I can not see the real sky.

Now here are some pictures
   of children playing.
A boy laughing through yellow fog,
tiger-coloured: his skin is gold,
         if gold could breathe.
His eyes, black
      lakes with moons inside.
The little girls of four and five
in their short dresses
squat so you see their white underwear.
By the time they are ten
their skirts are long enough
to hide their thighs.
Sometimes the men
cannot help smiling at the little ones
who walk up bold and curious, the children
who gaze long at the camera.

Oranges and Lemons

The second time
I came alone to say
a farewell of sorts, I wanted one more
look at her handwriting.

I was prepared for solitude, a floating
amputated quietness circling my wrists –
but not this song, not this

Oranges and lemons
Sold for a penny
All the schoolgirls
Are so many...

They rush in breathless
climbing up behind me, ahead of me, up
the warehouse steep Dutch staircase
to Anne Frank's room.
Schoolgirls, mostly schoolgirls
ages 13-16, they whisper about the important
things – staring everywhere: at windows, corners,
the ceiling. Staring at the paper,
her patient paper, her brown ink.
And a few linger behind, preferring to squint through
the netting, as if expecting something to happen
down by the other houses, the trees –

The grass is green
The rose is red
Remember me
When I am dead...

And a few linger behind, whispering
about the important things.

The Women of Leh are such –
for Jürgen Dierking

The women of Leh are such –
that one night over there, some 3,600 metres
high, not far from Tibet,
where the Zanskar glitters all day,
and at night, the stars, not to be outdone,
seem to grow larger, let themselves sink down closer
to the mountains – while the moon always disappears
by midnight, cut off by the horizon,
always on the other side
of some huge rock – one night
in that place I dreamt
and I saw Gertrude Stein selling
horseradishes and carrots. There was no mistaking
those shoulders – but she fit in so well
with her looking-straight-at-you eyes.
And yet, even the traditional
Ladakhi hat she wore could not disguise
her face. She said *jooley* to my *jooley*
with the others, all lined up along the main street –
she slapped the head of a hungry
rowdily exploring *dzo*
and I walked back, several times, back and forth,
pretending I couldn't decide what to buy.
Then she turned aside to talk with the tomato seller,
still keeping an eye on the *dzo* – it was hard to believe
but there was no mistaking that poise.

Paper and Glass

Kite-paper-blue sky
and the inky blue sea
can't stand it, sloshes up,
spills on, spits at and shreds
the paper sky.
And the sky droops down, drags
in the anger spinning sea.
And I watch dizzy
with dreams of you.
Dizzy, for there's nothing to drink.

At first, I feared snakes.
But there are only skeletons of fish,
slivers of glass and seashells.
Seaweed dries fast,
turning feathery, then leaping up to catch the wind.

I grow dizzy
without fresh water, without you,
I simply watch dolphins
zig-zagging
stitching the horizon in place.

Another Act for the Lübecker Totentanz

Bubble gum pink, rubber duck pink tulips
with petals half open like perfect page-boys
with petals that never fully opened –
so what a relief when after an entire week
they finally begin to wither.

At first a slow spiralling out,
a violet streaking through
then, a rush of coiling tentacles in every direction –
maroon and blue fur, furry orange stamens fermenting
peat with basil and thyme fragrance difficult to breathe maroon
powdery furry fragrance.
Not tulips anymore, not even dying tulips
but giant snapdragons gone haywire,
angry starfish trying to hatch something different.

What Is Worth Knowing?

That Van Gogh's ear, set free
wanted to meet the powerful nose
of Nevsky Avenue.
That Spain has decided to help
NATO. That Spring is supposed to begin
on the 21st of March.
That if you put too much salt in the *keema*
just add a few bananas.
That although the Dutch were the first
to help the people of Nicaragua they don't say much
about their history with Indonesia.
That Van Gogh collected Japanese prints.
That the Japanese considered
the Dutch to be red-haired barbarians.
That Van Gogh's ear remains full of questions
it wants to ask the nose of Nevsky Avenue.
That the vaccinations for cholera, typhoid and yellow fever
are no good – they must be improved.
That red, green and yellow are the most
auspicious colours.
That turmeric and chilli powder are good
disinfectants. Yellow and red.
That often Spring doesn't come
until May. But in some places
it's there in January.
That Van Gogh's ear left him because
it wanted to become a snail.
That east and west
meet only in the north and south – but never
in the east or west.
That in March 1986 Darwinism is being
reintroduced in American schools.
That there's a difference
between pigeons and doves, although
a ring-dove is a wood-pigeon.
That the most pleasant thing is to have a fever
of at least 101 – because then the dreams aren't
merely dreams but facts.

That during a fever the soul comes out
for fresh air, that during a fever the soul bothers to
speak to you.
That tigers are courageous and generous-hearted
and never attack unless provoked –
but leopards,
leopards are malicious and bad-tempered.
That buffaloes too,
water-buffaloes that is, have a short temper.
That a red sky at night is a good sign for sailors,
for sailors... what is worth knowing?
What is worth knowing?

Another Day in Iowa City
for Andrei Voznesensky

"My father's been to your country," I begin.
But you interrupt, saying you want to go
to India... while I wonder
how your shirt is the same blue
as the blue dresses painted on
the glossy wooden Russian dolls
my father brought home one day.

Your shirt brought back
memories of my mother angry
at the government
for sending all our bananas to Russia.
Sturdy memories of Russian dolls and no bananas –
no bananas
but Russian dolls, one inside the other endlessly –
and the last doll, always my favourite,
a hard seed, a bright secret that would never open
although I could look through those small
small black eyes.

Tonight
how I focused on your shirt, your emphatic hands.
How I listened to you with snow falling, with snow
covering all the tired hoof-prints in my soul
I can not explain – and my noisy dreams
of Akaky Akakyvich searching for his overcoat
would make you laugh.

There's no way I could've told you
all this in public, in ten how-do-you-do minutes.

So later, when you paused to ask me:
"Don't you want to visit my country?"
with such questioning sadness –
I was ready to take off my shoes, ready to jump out
of the car, let's go, I wanted to say, let's go for a walk,
let's go for a swim, let's take the next flight out of here.

Living with Trains

Wherever I go
there are trains burning through my fingers.

These are the days of green light, insane lime green.

First there's the hot silence on railroad tracks
just after the train has whistled by rushing on.

And the lime-green light is tangled and woven through
the train's whistle.

That's the silence I want between my eyes.

Then there's the smell of old trains, old metal, old narrow tracks,
heavy male sweat and that smell of tar and coals burning rubber
and matches that go into the smell of this train's whistle
on lime-green hours.

That's the smell creeping into my silences.

Then there's the hushed riddle of old towns, the names don't
     matter
but try to choose a continent where the trains are still themselves.

On summer nights the train's whistle wants to make you sooty
wants to make a sooty dance through your silence.

Can't you take the soot, don't you like this soot?

Well, have some sooty birds and some sooty water too.
Don't misunderstand. I used to climb the rooftops
balancing on the burning noon shingles just to watch
the trains go by.
The soot on my eyelids elegant as piano black.

Elegant as a dance of lithe black sheep dogs, young sprigs and
     sharp teeth
through insane lime green.

Wherever I go
there are trains burning through my fingers.

Those wooden benches in the second class
compartment grimy with soot and sweat and filled
with the tired smell of hungry children. That's the noise
rushing beneath my eyelids. And the train's whistle
is tangled and woven through.

What is this sound this colour this smell
that cuts up my feet?
Walking along the tracks forever for no reason.

How can the smell of tar be so comforting?
And the noise of wheels on tracks and sun on tracks
and sharp cinders slapped through wind loving windows.

And this train, this *Deccan Queen* leans into the mountain leans
lullabying into my brain. Lanterns flashing fireflies
whistling on deeper into the mountain spiralling
up through my brain.

Wherever I go
there are trains burning through my fingers.

Children running up and down the train screaming
while the train slid through caves, rocking and slipping
down and the train scream darkening while
children run up and down.

Then Aaji was waiting at the station with fresh
ivory-coloured milk in a real milk-can.
We had to change tracks, get on another train but we drank
the milk in sleepy gulps on the empty dawn platform
while trains gurgled and wheels sneezed and whistles
curled up mute and tight.

All afternoon we counted telephone poles and mango trees
and crows. And the children selling berries: *jambus*
and *bors* at the village stations. All afternoon
we counted the stations.

It was in East Berlin that all the trains reminded me
of all the trains in India. Old wood,
old paint, old tracks drumming against wheels.

And the whole time I wanted to take photographs (forbidden)
of these railway stations. Later
as we stared at the cemented land
it grew dark, the wind kicked slowly
and the trees on Unter den Linden smelled of 1966 Ahmedabad.

We turned sniffing, sniffing, surprised and
circling the wind until I jumped to grab some Linden leaves.

Aaji, in my dreams why do you
still walk along the old railroad tracks by the Ahmedabad textile-mill
holding my mother's hand?

Baltimore

I'm still living in that evening
when the air around the bushes was greyish purple,
the hedges drooping like thirsty blood-hounds –
no flowers, nothing lovely as I walked
and walked, the dry grass choking
and rasping, poked through my sandals,
here and there a few green lawns.
Well now it's summer I thought,
so let me do something new I thought.
There was nothing lovely,

then the fireflies swirled out,
          lime and mustard sparks
streaking only the lucky blades of grass.

For the rest of that summer I waited
for everything – the rest of that summer
spiralled into one dry evening;
the rest of that summer
I understood less and less
while loving Kierkegaard more and more
and waiting, always waiting
for something that should be,
something I wanted to be
as sudden as fireflies.

The Woodcut

For days
I touch the block of pine wood,
pressing its hard edge
            against my forehead.

Uncertain for days
        while it rains
I walk through wet pine needles.
Water-softened pine cones
            flatten under my feet.

I follow the crooked
            wrenched roots,
past torn clumps of moss,
blue-grey feathers, white wisps of cat fur,
and everywhere the sticky leaves,
yellow leaves
            like the sliced skin of frogs
cover fallen logs, cover a squirrel's skull.

For days I touch
            the block of pine wood,
pressing its hard edge
            between my breasts.

Then remembering your harshness

I cut the first quick stroke
            sharp in the wood.

The Puppets
for Yeats, Hannes and Jutta

The puppets on every window-sill, every shelf
in the puppet-maker's house
are waiting patiently, urgently,
they're thinking of the cradle –
especially the two in the corner,
the woman growing out of and in to
the honest-looking man
who stands like a great wave, a great snake's hood behind her.
This miracle they've seen before
about to be repeated, this miracle they've tried
to follow in their minds... for the first time
they feel trapped.
If only the skin around their souls would tear open.
They're not afraid of the splinters, the chipped paint –
because wood-groans, like whale sounds, already
move deep through their whorls.
If only they could follow
the miracle with more than their minds,
with more than memories of watery roots
with more than the patience
or wisdom that came with metamorphosis
with more than following, more than copying
the puppet-maker and his wife –
No. They must find their own miracle.

Pink Shrimps and Guesses

Hey, are you there
already,   already
am I your mother?

Today I tried
to imagine your nose,
your eyebrows,
the shape your legs will take.
Whether you'll climb trees easily,
whether you'll cry easily.

Today I wanted you
to talk to me.
Tell me what you want.
Tell me, because I don't know.
Give me a hint at least.
When I look at the sky
can you smell the birds?
When I slip does your heart
beat faster? Do you like
red peppers? When I hear the birds
can you taste the sun on their feathers?
Tell me what you want.
Shall we meet face to face
in nine months, shall we?
Or would you rather forget about it?
I want to ask you
how it feels in there.
Do you mind if I run,
what are you thinking,
do my dreams keep you awake,
do I taste good already,
can you trust me?

Looking Over What I Have Done

I am kind to some
of these poems only because
I wrote them when you were still here.

Hey,

your photographs
of Indian temples are incomplete.
Where's that man I saw every day
                laughing
at the clean
Brahmin's children
who were afraid of him?
Where's that man
with the swollen elephant leg
     who sits by the pillar
              crawling with gods and flies?

Search For My Tongue*

Days my tongue slips away.
I can't hold on to my tongue.
It's slippery like the lizard's tail
I try to grasp
but the lizard darts away.

મારી જીભ સરકી જાય છે
(mari jeebh sarki jai chay)
I can't speak. I speak nothing.
Nothing.

કાં ઇ નહિ, હું નથી બોલી શકતી
(kai nahi, hoo nathi boli shakti)
I search for my tongue.

પરંતુ ક્યાં શોધું ? ક્યાં ?
(parantu kya shodhu? Kya?)

હું દોડતી દોડતી જાઉં છું.
(hoo dhodti dhodti jaoo choo)
But where should I start? Where?
I go running, running,

નદી કિનારે પહોંચી છું, નદી કિનારે.
(nadi keenayray pohchee choo, nadi keenayray)
reach the river's edge.
Silence

એકદમ શાંત.
(akedum shant)

નીચે પાણી નહિ, ઉપ્પર પક્ષી નહિ.
(neechay pani nahi, oopur pakshi nahi)
Below, the riverbed is dry. Above,
the sky is empty: no clouds, no birds.
If there were leaves, or even grass
they would not stir today,
for there is no breeze.
If there were clouds
then, it might rain.

*The Gujerati is translated into English within the poem itself.

જે વાદળ હોત તો કદાચ વરસાદ આવે,
(jo vadla hoat toh kadach varsad aavay)

જે વરસાદ પડે તો નદી પાછી આવે,
(jo varsad puday toh nadi pachee aavay)

જે નદી હોય, જે પાણી હોય, તો કાંઈક લીલું લીલું દેખાય.
(jo nadi hoy, jo pani hoy, toh kaeek leelu leelu daykhai)
If the rains fell
then the river might return,
if the water rose again I might see something green
at first, then trees enough to fill a forest.
If there were some clouds that is.

જે વાદળા હોત તો.
(jo vadla hoat toh)
Since I have lost my tongue
I can only imagine
there is something crawling
beneath the rocks, now burrowing down
into the earth when I lift the rock.

જ્યારે પથ્થર ઉપાડું.
(jyaray patther oopadu)
The rock is in my hand, and the dry
moss stuck on the rock
prickles my palm.
I let it drop
for I must find my tongue.
I know it can't be here
in this dry riverbed.
My tongue can only be
where there is water.

પાણી, પાણી,
(pani, pani)

હજુ યાદ છે પેલી છોકરી.
(hujoo yad chay paylee chokri)

"ઠંડા પાણી, મીઠા પાણી," બોલતી બોલતી આવતી.
("thunda pani, meetha pani, bolti bolti aavti)

64

માથે કાળું માટલું , હાથમાં પીત્તળનો પ્યાલો.
(mathay kallu matlu, hathma pittulno pyalo)

ઉભેલી ગાડી બાજુ આવતી.
(oobhaylee gaadi baju aavti)

બારી તરફ હાથ લંબાવીને પાણી આપતી.
(bari taraf hath lumbaveenay pani aapti)

અને હું , અતિશય તરસી,
(unay hoo, ateeshay tarsi)

મોટા મોટા ઘૂં ટડા લેતી પી જતી.
(mota mota ghuntada layti pee jati)

હજુ યાદ છે પેલી છોકરી.
(hujoo yad chay paylee chokri)
Even water is scarce.
There was a little girl
who carried a black clay pitcher on her head,
who sold water at the train station.
She filled her brass cup with water,
stretched out her arm to me,
reached up to the window, up
to me leaning out the window from the train,
but I can't think of her in English.

II

You ask me what I mean
by saying I have lost my tongue.
I ask you, what would you do
if you had two tongues in your mouth,
and lost the first one, the mother tongue,
and could not really know the other,
the foreign tongue.
You could not use them both together
even if you thought that way.
And if you lived in a place you had to
speak a foreign tongue,
your mother tongue would rot,
rot and die in your mouth

until you had to spit it out.
I thought I spit it out
but overnight while I dream,

મને હતું કે આખ્ખી જીભ આખ્ખી ભાષા,
(munay hutoo kay aakhee jeebh aakhee bhasha)

મેં થૂં કી નાખી છે.
(may thoonky nakhi chay)

પરં તુ રાત્રે સ્વપ્નામાં મારી ભાષા પાછી આવે છે.
(parantoo rattray svupnama mari bhasha pachi aavay chay)

ફુલની જેમ મારી ભાષા મારી જીભ
(foolnee jaim mari bhasha mari jeebh)

મોઢામાં ખીલે છે.
(modhama kheelay chay)

ફૂલની જેમ મારી ભાષા મારી જીભ
(fulllnee jaim mari bhasha mari jeebh)

મોઢામાં પાકે છે.
(modhama pakay chay)
it grows back, a stump of a shoot
grows longer, grows moist, grows strong veins,
it ties the other tongue in knots,
the bud opens, the bud opens in my mouth,
it pushes the other tongue aside.
Everytime I think I've forgotten,
I think I've lost the mother tongue,
it blossoms out of my mouth.
Days I try to think in English:
I look up,

પેલો કાળો કાગડો
(paylo kallo kagdo)

ઉડતો ઉડતો જાય, હવે ઝાડે પહોંચે,
(oodto oodto jai, huhvay jzaday pohchay)

એની ચાં ચમાં કાં ઇક છે.
(ainee chanchma kaeek chay)
the crow has something in his beak.
When I look up

I think:

આકાશ, સુરજ
(aakash, suraj)
and then: sky, sun.
Don't tell me it's the same, I know
better. To think of the sky
is to think of dark clouds bringing snow,
the first snow is always on Thanksgiving.
But to think:

આકાશ, અસમાન, આભ.
(aakash, usman, aabh)
માથે મોટા કાળા કાગડા ઉડે.
(mathay mota kalla kagda ooday)
કાગડાને માથે સુરજ, રોજે સુરજ.
(kagdanay mathay suraj, rojjay suraj)
એકપણ વાદળ નહિ, એટલે વરસાદ નહિ,
(akepun vadul nahi, atelay varsad nahi)
એટલે અનાજ નહિ, એટલે રોટલી નહિ,
(atelay anaj nahi, atelay rotli nahi)
દાળ ભાત શાક નહિ, કાં ઇ નહિ, કુછ ભી નહિ,
(dal bhat shak nahi, kai nahi, kooch bhi nahi)

માત્ર કાગડા, કાળા કાગડા.
(matra kagda, kalla kagda)
Overhead, large black crows fly.
Over the crows, the sun, always
the sun, not a single cloud
which means no rain, which means no wheat,
no rice, no greens, no bread. Nothing.
Only crows, black crows.
And yet, the humid June air,
the stormiest sky in Connecticut
can never be

આકાશ
(aakash)

ચોમાસામાં જ્યારે વરસાદ આવે
(chomasama jyaray varsad aavay)

આખ્ખી રાત આખ્ખો દિ' વરસાદ પડે, વિજળી જાય,
(aakhee raat aakho dee varsad puday, vijli jai)

જ્યારે મા રસોડામાં ઘીને દીવે રોટલી વણતી
(jyaray ma rasodama gheenay deevay rotli vanti)

શાક હલાવતી
(shak halavti)

રવિંદ્ર સંગીત ગાતી ગાતી
(Ravindrasangeet gaati gaati)

સૌને બોલાવતી
(saonay bolavti)
the monsoon sky giving rain
all night, all day, lightning, the electricity goes out,
we light the cotton wicks in butter:
                candles in brass.
And my mother in the kitchen,
my mother singing:

મોન મોર મેઘેર શંગે ઉડે ચોલે દિગ્દિગંતેર પાને . . .
(mon mor megher shungay, ooday cholay dikdigontair panay)
I can't hear my mother in English.

III

In the middle of Maryland
you send me a tape-recording
saying "હવે આ એક વાત તો કહેવી જ પડશે,
                (huhvay aa ake vat toh kahveej padshay)

ભલેને બહાર કૂતરા ભસે, ભલે ધોબી આવે,
(bhalaynay bahr kootra bhasay, bhalay dhobi aavay)

ભલે શાકવાળી આવે, મારે આ વાત તો કહેવી જ પડશે.
(bhalay shakvali aavay, maray aa vat toh kahveej padshay)

ભલે ટપાલી આવે, ભલે કાગડા કો કો કરે,
(bhalay tapali aavay, bhalay kagda kaw kaw karay)

ભલે રીકશાનો અવાજ આવે,
(bhalay rickshano avaj aavay)

મારે તને આ વાત તો કહેવી જ પડશે''.
(maray tanay aa vat toh kahveej padshay)
You talk to me,
    you say my name the way it should be said,
apologising
for the dogs barking outside
for the laundryman knocking on the door,
apologising because
the woman selling eggplants

is crying   રીંગણા, રીંગણા   door to door
        (reengna, reengna)
But do you know
how I miss that old woman, crying   રીંગણા, રીંગણા
                    (reengna, reengna)
It's all right if the pedlar's brass bells ring out,
I miss them too.
You talk louder, the mailman comes, knocking louder,
the crows caw-caw-cawing outside,
the rickshaw's motor put-put-puttering.

You say સુજુ બેન હવે તમારે માટે તબલા વગાડું છું.
        (Suju bhen huhvay tamaray matay tabla vagadu choo)
you say: listen to the tablas,
listen:

ધા ધીન ધીન ધા	(dha dhin dhin dha)
ધા ધીન ધીન ધા	(dha dhin dhin dha)
listen ધા ધીન ધીન ધા	(dha dhin dhin dha)
ધીનક ધીનક ધીન ધીન	(dhinaka dhinaka dhin dhin)
ધીનક ધીનક ધીન ધીન	(dhinaka dhinaka dhin dhin)
ધા ધીન ધીન ધા	(dha dhin dhin dha)
ધીનક ધીનક ધીનક ધીનક	(dhinaka dhinaka dhinaka dhinaka)
ધા ધીન ધીન ધા	(dha dhin dhin dha)
ધીનક ધીનક ધીન ધીન	(dhinaka dhinaka dhin dhin)

69

I listen I listen I listen

ધા ધીન ધીન ધા   (dha dhin dhin dha)

   I hear you I hear you

ધીનક ધીનક ધીન ધીનક ધીનક ધીન ધીનક ધીનક ધીન
(dhinaka dhinaka dhin dhinaka dhinaka dhin dhinaka dhinaka dhin)
     listen   listen   listen
Today I played your tape
over and over again

      ધા ધીન ધીન ધા   (dha dhin dhin dha)

       ધીનક ધીનક ધા   (dhinaka dhinaka dha)

                  I can't   ધા   (dha)

I can't   ધા   (dha)

I can't forget   I can't forget

      ધા ધીન ધીન ધા   (dha dhin dhin dha)

III

Eurydice Speaks

Marie Curie to Her Husband

The equations are luminous now.
They glimmer across my page,
across the walls
across the pillow
where your forehead should be.
You would've smiled at the shape of your graph
which I completed test tube by test tube.

You've managed to slip inside me,
managed to curl your length tightly within my chest.
I want to remind you
of periwinkles, narcissus,
wisteria, iris, laburnum;
the cows that plodded over to sniff,
the handlebars we clutched while bicycling past so many trees,
so many skies and grasses.
Reaching shelter in the dark, each night we'd go
inspect our magic lights, glowing hot
yellow and green, yellow and blue,
caught in rows and rows of bottles.

I now crave grey,
crave rain: days like the one
that killed you keep me
in the laboratory and the lecture halls.
Pierre, this afternoon at one thirty
I continued your lecture at the Sorbonne.
This afternoon
you tossed around in my chest.
Your beard streamed in my veins, my blood. You thrashed,
your legs knocking against my ribs
while I analysed the progress
that has been made in physics.
But at night, I still count in Polish.

Clara Westhoff to Rainer Maria Rilke

No road leads
to this old house we chose.
Its roof of straw scattered
by the loud wind wheezing
its North Sea sounds.
No road leads
to this old house we chose.

I live downstairs
with my clay and stones.
You upstairs
with ink and paper.
What do we do but play with truth,
a doll whose face
I must rework again and again
until it is human.
The clay has gathered all the warmth
from my hands. I am too cold
to touch the marble yet.

Last night the wind blew
my candle out. Tonight again
on the staircase, I
grope my way to your room.
Each night I climb
up these steps
back to you, with your open windows
so close to the wind and stars.
I listen to your poems as I wash
the dust off my skin and hair.
You must have the windows open all night,
I must watch
the straw from the roof
slowly swirl, fall inside
and gently cover your poems.

Tomorrow
come downstairs, will you,
it has been a month.
I want to show you
the new stone I found
stuck in the mud by the dead tree.
Such a smooth globe, not quite white
but honeydew
with a single dark green vein curled across.
Come downstairs, will you, see
the bright red leaves I stole from the woods;
see my lopsided clay
figure bow low down
before my untouched marble.
Tomorrow
come see the ground,
the gawky yellow weeds
at eye level from my window down below.

For Paula Modersohn-Becker
(1876-1907)

The way I returned again and again to your self-portrait with blue
    irises
made the guards uneasy.

The way I turned away from your self-portrait with blue irises
made the guards uneasy.

Was it the blue irises floating around your face, was it
your brown eyes illuminated by something in the blue irises?

How could you know, how could you feel all this
that I know and feel about blue iris?

I was on the top floor with other paintings, other painters,
but unable to concentrate on them because
already I could hear the tone of voice your brown eyes would
    require.

So I rushed back down to be with you.

The look that passed between us must have lasted
a long time because I could smell the light
from the irises falling across your face.

The look that passed between us was full
of understanding so I could imagine living with you
and arguing with you about whether to put garlic in the soup.

I stared at the blue irises but in my throat
there was the pungent fresh bitterness of watercress.

When I finally left you I noticed three guards following me.

By the time I got home I was furious at them
for witnessing all this.

The Garlic of Truth

છમ છમ વઘાર
(cham cham vaghar)

રાઇ મેથી લસણ ધીમાં લઢે . . .
(rai methi lasann gheema ladhay...)
Mustard seeds popping in hot butter,
crushed garlic whispering urgent, pungent messages
while fenugreek seeds help amber the butter.
Today I use a wooden spoon
turmeric stained,
we let the garlic take over the house before
opening the windows. Let the mustard seeds fly
as far as they dare – days later
we might find some on the sofa.
Days later the roof will wake up breathing garlic.

છમ છમ વઘાર
(cham cham vaghar)

રાઇ મેથી લસણ ધીમાં લઢે . . .
(rai methi lasann gheema ladhay...)
The crooked insect broke its legs
inside my ear while
ma strained garlic pulp out of the herbal oil
before she poured it warm-thickly down my ear
and put me to dream with sleep.
Oh that sleep with garlicked oil in my ear
gave me such dreamy truth, such truthful dreams.

Once upon a time, truth stood with a capital 'T'
like this: Truth.
When people laughed the 'T' slumped and wished
it were part of an undiscovered tiger instead.
Not that anyone knew
what it meant: Truth or truth, big deal.

Thatched roof, peat smell all the way down my shirt.
If there were thoughts

77

in my head I didn't know it.
Bicycle wheels want to try forever.
Indigoed wet bog-land light, the same light
curled inside my hair, the same
light beneath the cow's tongue.

Prayag swallows a clove of garlic every day.
A single clove
every day a strong crescent...
but this may not work for you.

And Truth went indigo with the clouds,
and Truth went inside the smoking peat that didn't
finish burning.

Don't you need more garlic?
But this can't be enough!
Oh let me peel some more 'cause I'm itching
to take off all the rice paper cocoon skins
because now I'm in the mood to sliver garlic slices all day.

So this is the land and this is the light
I described so precisely five years ago without once
seeing it. And here is the North Sea
to make sure I stay surprised.

Paula Becker would you have dared to try garlic?

The true Jains, the true Brahmins,
the orthodox-orthodox prefer truth without garlic.

But you
funny how you got such pleasure
after work, shoes off, no shirt,
chopping up garlic while listening to the news
while I kneaded chapati dough...

Wanting Agni

1

She lies beneath marigolds, tulsi, roses and roses
beneath the shade of a neem tree whose leaves
have fallen over the roses over her – Then,
it's time she's carried out
on a bed of bamboo: a *kathi*
that's more like a crooked ladder.
The roses and roses and neem leaves
still scattered over her –
By now she's just like dry wood, her long straight legs
the same neem-wood colour and her heart
which is beginning to smell, is turning dark,
is turning into the neem-bitter-sour smell.

There are six young men
with thick hair always falling in their eyes,
six young men with enough muscle to please
who carry the *kathi* high on their shoulders.
So high that I don't even see her
white sari bundled up shape underneath which she is becoming
neem, neem green and brown.

Not allowed to watch I watched thinking,
that's how I want to leave one day.

The six young men keep walking beyond the neem trees,
beyond the trails into some open and useless field.
They keep walking with their heads held still and high
despite all the hair falling into their eyes.
They walk a rocking smooth and lilting walk,
an elephant rolling walk that cradles her
as she turns into the smell of neem trees.

Not allowed to follow I followed thinking,
that's how I want to become one day.

If they want to bury me
my scalp will be afraid,
if they do an autopsy
my soul will be stuck in the fluorescent lights
watching
watching with hydrochloric acid-shame and embarrassment.
But if I'm taken away on bamboo and roses and neem
and placed on more wood
then Agni, the good god of fire will come rushing towards me,
    laughing
as if tickled by all the saffron.
The same Agni who would not touch the fire-strong and pure
Sita, returns again and again –
The same Agni, worshipped by prostitutes in Bombay
as they cleanse themselves, leaping
over flames between customers –
That Agni returns again and again
even for me.

3

I came to look at Paula Becker's grave
but spent more time staring down at a freshly dug-up pit,
a new hole waiting for someone.
You said you want to be buried further north, close to the sea.
I said nothing but tried to think of the most beautiful –
a delicately cut, licked and embroidered
by moonflowers and sunflowers gravestone for you.

4

It's when I walk past graveyards
and walk through graveyards or when I see
peat preserved humans in books and museums
that I long for the neem trees of Poona
the fresh bitter green and salt smell
sometimes just like the smell on the wet hair under your arms –
yes the warm hair behind your ears smells

of neem after I kiss you there and there
and pull you deep inside there where you and I begin
to smell of crushed neem leaves.
So the tall gravestones insisting
that we pause a little make me stop
and wish for a neem tree, and wish
I'll burn with fragrant wood – these tall gravestones
make me look at the trees.

Eurydice Speaks

Orpheus, I tell you I'm not in hell,
this place is called Maine.
All winter the cold wind burns my face,
and I sweat, wading through all this snow.
But it's spring now:
sounds of snow melting,
water dripping off eaves, flooding crocuses
and jack-in-the-pulpits.
Pussy willows, cattails, forsythia suddenly
awaken junipers tipped with pale new shoots.
The wind flings pine cones my way.
Now walking along the coast
I follow seagulls
with my camera, seagulls
skimming waves and I focus
on their bills in the foaming
water, they dip their bills,
I focus, they rise with limp silver
flashing in the sun as others come swooping
down, I turn circling with my camera
while waves rise and crash upon rocks
flinging salty seaweed and mollusks;
chipping seashells upon cliffs
waves crash and leave small pools of fish stranded...
Orpheus, I want to stay here
with the smooth pebbles,
I want to stay here, at the ocean's edge
I have found someone new –
no god, but a quiet man who listens.

Mein lieber Schwan

Everyone must keep away –
don't come too close, don't touch it
because your fingers are too thick.
Your blistered fingers will snarl the silken eyelids
smudge the colours, smear the light,
your sweaty fingers will suffocate
the gently breathing idea.
So Psyche learned, so Elsa learned.

Psyche, Elsa –
I see them long-necked, long-haired
and quite fed up –
ready to change into rivers, birds, anything –
ready to look for a new country, anything
to keep from turning around with questioning hands,
always moving as if they were swimming
as if the wind were contantly blowing around them.

Psyche, Elsa –
They who were most unconscious
as if their minds were overflowing with truth,
they who seemed to have no questions
couldn't help probing

just as young Wagner
sincere anarchist, yes
Wagner, a *sincere anarchist*,
dreamed of one nation bound with violins
curled around trumpets curled around young
white necks curled around thick swords
curled around blue ribbons, red roses,
and feathers, feathers to cushion every fall.

Written After Hearing about the
Soviet Invasion of Afghanistan

Here,
a child born
in winter
    rarely survives.
Bibi Jamal's son died.
She pounds hard dough,
kneads in yak milk, quickly kneads in fat,
rolls the dough out round and flat.
Her older co-wife cooks the bread.
Bibi Jamal can't speak of it yet.

It's cold enough. Birds have come inside.
Her co-wife sleeps, thick feet
by the fire in the yurt's centre.
On the fire's other side Bibi Jamal weaves
diagrams of Darjeeling into a carpet:
    Hills sprouting tea-leaves, rivers in froth down mountains,
    and there must be red, she feels,
    red skirts flowing through fields,
    ripe pomegranates broken open in some garden.
    With such green
    with such blue Himalayan sky
                there's always red.

Nothing like
the granite, treeless
mountains she knows.

Bibi Jamal's thread never breaks,
even as she dreams of Darjeeling.
And her husband, already on the Hindu Kush,
doesn't know how her breasts ache with milk.

She can include
    his voice slicing through miserable gusts;
    caravanserai well-water strawberry on his tongue.
    So she listens: snow visits,

84

her husband pitches his black tent.
She spots nearby
a slouched snow-leopard.
It moves, makes her jump,
stops for a minute, noses the air, steals
away through sharp sword grass.
Her husband remains
safe in his black tent.
He'll be beyond the Khyber pass soon.
She draws green thread through her fingers.

2

What do you know of Bibi Jamal?
Her husband, napalmed,
ran burning across the rocks.
Crisp shreds of skin, a piece of his turban,
a piece of his skull were delivered to her.
She only stared, didn't understand,
muttered, "Allah Allah Allah Allah is great. But,
where is my husband? Allah Allah Allah."
She'll ask you when she understands.

3 November 1984

I won't buy
The New York Times today.
I can't. I'm sorry.
But when I walk into the bookstore
I can't help reading the front page
and I stare at the photographs
of dead men and women
I know I've seen alive.

Today I don't want to think
of Hindus cutting open
Sikhs – and Sikhs cutting open
Hindus – and Hindus cutting open

Today I don't want to think
of Amrit and Arun and Gunwant Singh,
nor of Falguni and Kalyan.

I've made up my mind: today I'll write
in peacock-greenish-sea-green ink I'll write
poems about everything else.
I'll think of the five Americans
who made it
to Annapurna without Sherpa help.
I won't think of haemorrhageing trains
I'll get my homework done.

Now instead of completing this poem
I'm drawing imlee fronds
all over this page
and thinking of Amrit when we were six
beneath the imlee tree
his long hair just washed
just as long as my hair just washed.
Our mothers sent us outside in the sun
                    to play, to dry our hair.
Now instead of completing this poem
I'm thinking of Amrit.

You Walk into This Room and

Look how you turned on
the ceiling fan – it's too high,
see how it shakes and trembles.
You walk into this room
with your hot ideas
and the ceiling fan has to work harder
to cool down the room
for us. You walk into this room
with your crazy eyes
and the ceiling fan
wants to fly loose. It dreams
of becoming a spider lily.

Mappelmus

How I enjoyed
missing you today
walking through the rain
and not wanting
an umbrella
through puddles and slushing
yes, sliding through *Mappelmus*
how I enjoyed
missing you today
while drinking tea
and washing out pantyhose –
everything and I
the colour of *Mappelmus*.
Come back soon
but how I enjoyed
missing you today.

The Undertow

There are at least three
languages between us.
And the common space, the common dream-sound
is far out at sea.
There's a certain spot, dark
far out where the waves sleep
there's a certain spot
we always focus on,
and the three languages are there
swimming like seals fat with fish and sun
they smile, the three languages
understand each other so well.

We stand watching, jealous
of the three languages, wishing
we could swim so easily.
But the waves keep us back,
the undertow threatens;
so we take one word at a time.
Take 'dog' for example,

કૂતરો   (kootro) in Gujarati, *Köter* in Low German
Hund in High German, like hound in English.

Dog   કૂતરો   (kootro)   *Köter*   *Hund*

hound   *dog*   *Köter*   કૂતરો   (kootro)

કૂતરો   કૂતરો   કૂતરો
(kootro   kootro   kootro)

The waves come chasing
the dogs on the beach
the waves come flooding the streets
listen to the seals swimming
through the bookstores, listen
the words spill together,

the common sounds:
ક ખ ગ

    શ ક્ષ સ

kö   kh   ga

    sh   ksh   ß   spill together

spill together
filling our shoes,
    filling our love with salt.

At the Marketplace

Look at the young jade-coloured artichokes!
Shall we have some for dinner?
Yes? No?
But wait. Look, there's fish in the next stall –
Oh to eat raw fish and raw onions and fresh
lemon juice and more raw fish –
juicy salt.
Eating raw fish
it doesn't matter if it's raining –
cold, and the umbrella
is blown aside – Eating raw fish
makes you feel like a mermaid through your legs –
Juicy salt.
I always crave sea salt, sour salt, strong eel salt.

Now there are purple sea horses all over her
and she is becoming a mermaid with artichoke skin.
Purple sea horses that he branded last night –
on her neck, shoulders, thighs: acrobatic purple,
elegant tattoo tails plunging deep into eel salt.
Sea horses are sucking on her salt
and she is talking like a mermaid, reasoning like a mermaid;
sea horses growing fuller and dark fat purple
and she eats another raw herring, swallowing
like a mermaid.

Metamorphoses II: A Dream
for Eleanor Wilner

Deep in the forests of New England:
Vermont, Maine? Somewhere over there
I lost the trail and wandered all day.
I circled around and around the hills.
Then, late in the afternoon,
the woods suddenly gave way
to a garden and a house.

As I knocked on the door
it opened to a dark hallway
which led to a room, marigold bright
with the afternoon sun. And there was a woman
in the middle of the room
surrounded by silk:
the green of grasshoppers at dawn,
the dun of horses and hay
beneath a blue hyacinth sky.

She sat hunched over her work.
The room, hushed, as if in awe
of her concentration.
And oh how the needle moved
like some delicate silver fish
it rushed swiftly through the waves in her hands.
I lingered by the doorway, watching,
not wanting to disturb her.

She weaves branches that move
with the shadows of birds.
Evergreen woods and ferns:
long fronds softly stir
and nudge lupine,
moist fronts invite a worm
to seek a home in there
while acorns the colour of acorns
roll down the hills of her tapestries.

92

Suddenly she looked up and smiled
as if she knew I'd be coming.
For a long time I sat beside her
watching, listening
to the mysterious silk which cannot be torn.
Watching it soft as a newborn
animal's naked skin
come alive in her hands; everything breathes
in the tapestry and someone whispers.

When I looked up again
I could see moths
fluttering against the window-pane.
"It is late," she said
as we gathered up the silk
"but you must come back tomorrow."

The second day she led me to her garden.
Beyond the familiar azalea
and blue phlox, the gooseberries
and mulberries, beyond the apple trees
there were tall vines
weighed down with golden eggplants.
Dark blue cauliflowers
fanning their elephant-ear leaves
against slender red asparagus,
orange lettuce, and oh, the bell peppers
had grown long white beards.
I stood there amazed
while she said: "Come look at the flowers growing
beside the pond. There's something
in the water over here
that makes them good to eat."

How can I describe this flower?
Some strange mix of lotus and rose:
The stem, poised like a dancer
waiting for the music to begin.
Leaves of a rose, only larger.
The thorns, longer

to match the sturdy lotus stalk,
and the flower
the size of a woman's head
slightly raised, petals open.

I, too, stood waiting
for the music to begin,
but she said "come on", pulling me along
as she filled a wide basket
she put into my hands.
Then, in the kitchen,
she brought out her knife,
(the blade a blur of silver)
she cut these fruits
into perfect circles, triangles,
ovals, hexagons – explaining how each one
had to be cut a certain way
because if it's cut the wrong way
it won't nourish us as well.
And then she showed me
how to remove the petals,
enormous, from the lotus-rose.
And how to serve wild black rice:
caviar from the earth
on a bed of purple-red petals.

Now each day I climb through the woods
to visit her. The path I make slowly
grows more visible. Each day
I learn how to hold the threads of silk:
taut yet slack enough for a supple weave.
And when our eyes tire towards dusk,
we go outside and water that garden
infused with the lotus-rose.

Saturday Night on Keswick Road

The children outside my window
are now louder than the traffic.
Motorbikes race by
     but the children laugh louder.

Inside
I'm trying to read,
inside
a freight train has fallen over
        the cliffs
and now burns. Does not stop burning.
The trees are also burning with my cargo.
I can smell the sweet green wood turn black
while I'm trying to read
the smoke hides the words
still, I'm trying to read.

But the children, the children,
their voices
     blow the cinders away
from my stinging eyes,
keep the rest of the mountain from burning.

The Writer

The best story, of course,
is the one you can't write,
        you won't write.
It's something that can only live
        in your heart,
not on paper.

Paper is dry, flat.
Where is the soil
for the roots, and how do I lift out
entire trees, a whole forest
from the earth of the spirit
and transplant it on paper
without disturbing the birds?

And what about the mountain
on which this forest grows?
The waterfalls
        making rivers,
rivers with throngs of trees
elbowing each other aside
to have a look
at the fish.

Beneath the fish
        there are clouds.
Here, the sky ripples,
the river thunders.
How would things move on paper?

Now watch   the way
                the tigers' walking
        shreds the paper.

Sad Songs with Henna Leaves

Sing me sad songs and I'll be happy
sing me happy songs and I'll be sad;
give me good-luck and I'll want to die
give me bad-luck and I'll live.

But I try to follow the *Bhagavad Gita*
where it says:
Become like the turtle.
When it is time to work use your eyes to see
and your ears to hear.
When your work is finished, withdraw your senses
and turn within.

But how can I
when the lines in my palms are getting deeper,
sharper, as if someone comes everyday
and secretly, bloodlessly, goes over them with a knife.
The lines in my palms are
getting deeper as if that means anything –
What do I believe? How can I say
that the patterns in my palms mean more
than they mean?

Sometimes,
we understand this world through दुःख (dukkha) –
Sanskrit word, Pali word,

दुःख   meaning sorrow

दुःख   meaning suffering, misery,

दुःख   meaning pain –

So Gautama Buddha said.

But   दुःख   also decorates her palms, colours my palms

with tiny henna leaves – dark red-veined
brown tendrils bind my fingers.

दुःख   even comes smelling of hot *chapatis*

and water sprinkled on dusty stones.

Tail

Meaningless black marks
cover my page, they stretch and grow
                    into a cat.

The cat demands trees,
a whole forest of wood to sharpen her claws,
                    and squirrels.

Black marks twist into branches,
tiny buds dot the twigs.
Three squirrels swirl up the trunk of an Oak.
The cat pretends her eyes are blind stones,
pretends she is a stone among stones.
The squirrels know and refuse to come out.
Then, it starts snowing
                    slowly
                    softly   large flakes
                                begin covering the black marks.

Go to Ahmedabad

Go walk the streets of Baroda,
go to Ahmedabad,
go breathe the dust
until you choke and get sick
with a fever no doctor's heard of.
Don't ask me
for I will tell you nothing
about hunger and suffering.

As a girl I learned
never to turn anyone away
from our door. Ma told me
give fresh water, good food,
nothing you wouldn't eat.
Hunger is when your mother
tells you years later
in America the doctor says
she is malnourished,
her bones are weak
because there was never enough
food for the children,
hers and the women who came
to our door with theirs.
The children must always be fed.
Hunger is when your mother is sick
in America because she wanted you
to eat well. Hunger is
when you walk
down the streets of Ahmedabad
and instead of handing out
coins to everyone
you give them tomatoes, cucumbers,
and go home with your mouth
tasting of burnt eucalyptus leaves
because you've lost
your appetite.
And yet, I say nothing
about hunger, nothing.

I have friends everywhere.
This time we met after ten years.
Someone died.
Someone got married.
Someone just had a baby.
And I hold the baby
because he's crying,
because there's a strange rash
all over his chest.
And my friend says
do you have a child? Why not?
When will you get married?
And the bus arrives
crowded with people hanging
out the doors and windows.
And her baby cries
in my arms, cries
so an old man wakes up and yells
at me: How could I let
my child get so sick?
Luckily, just then
someone tells a good joke.

I have friends everywhere.
This time we met after ten years.
And suffering is
when I walk around Ahmedabad
for this is the place
I always loved
this is the place
I always hated
for this is the place
I can never be at home in
this is the place
I will always be at home in.
Suffering is
When I'm in Ahmedabad
after ten years
and I learn for the first time
I will never choose

to live here. Suffering is
living in America
and not being able
to write a damn thing
about it. Suffering is
not for me to tell you about.

Go walk the streets of Baroda,
go to Ahmedabad
and step around the cow-dung
but don't forget
to look at the sky.
It's special in January,
you'll never see kites like these again.
Go meet the people if you can
and if you want to know
about hunger, about suffering,
go live it for yourself.
When there's an epidemic,
when the doctor says
your brother may die soon,
your father may die soon –
don't ask me how it feels.
It does not feel good.
That's why we make
tea with tulsi leaves,
that's why there's always someone
who knows a good story.

To My Muse

Come on, take off your turban,
let's lie in this field
of tall grass;   come on, take off your turban,
cover me with your softly flowing hair,
your long beard, let's sleep
                    face to face, mouth to mouth
in this field of yellow, violet veined flowers,
                    open-mouthed flowers.
        Let's sleep
deep within this tangled field.

"And the poems?" you ask.
I don't know, I let them go
            as they please.
Some have turned into water,
            the water that rains down
                    every monsoon,
            the water that turns
                    the earth green
                        every year.
"The poems?" you wonder.
Yes, some have turned into water.
Others, thick clusters of green bamboo
                    rain drenched
the slender shoots, the long leaves
            so wet   and the ground
reddish brown
        earth-worms swollen with rain water
coil and uncoil, twist and reel
            in the mud
beneath the bamboo green.

And oh, how the wind comes to dance
            with the bamboo stalks,
        how the wind comes to sing
            with the bamboo leaves.

Listen, sounds almost like the rustle of Mysore silk.
Listen   rustling   somewhere
maybe a woman in Mysore silk
            is swirling faster, and faster
                        her sari billows out
while the bamboo tops
            nod yes, yes.

Come on, take off your turban,
and I'll comb out your hair.
"But the poems?" you insist.
I don't know I let them grow
            as they please.
Wanting the bamboo forest, thick
            the stalks, tall
wanting them green enough, strong enough
            for the wind –
even Krishna, Dionysus's older brother,
understood. Even Krishna-Govind-Govind-Gopal
said he wouldn't cut
a single stem for his flute.

Brunizem
for Michael

Brunizem, I say
and brummagem.
I have the jack of hearts
in my pocket – yes
he was waiting for me
on a shelf
in a thrift shop.
But he is more than the jack of hearts
and he kissed me.
I still keep the card
in my pocket.
Brummagem, I say
and brunizem.

The other night
I dreamt English
was my middle name.
And I cried, telling my mother
"I don't want English
to be my middle name.
Can't you change it to something else?"
"Go read the dictionary." She said.

I've been meaning
not to mean anything for once.
I just want to say, "brunizem!"
I feel brunizem
when this man kisses me
I want to learn another language.

Well, Well, Well,

How can I tell you about it
without using those words again?
I need words like *witch*, *power*,
maybe even *gypsy* – I don't know.
But I need *witch*. Will you grant me that?

Blood-salty egg yolks soft boiled 3 minutes,
the colour of Africa on my wall map.

These mornings it takes 5 minutes
to figure out where I am.

Sometimes bone-marrow is pure.
Pure and innocent and clean.
Sometimes bone-marrow is delicious.
Delicious and pure and innocent.
They taught the 4 year old girl
to suck out the young goat's fresh marrow.
After that she refused
to sleep alone.

When night spiders crawl on brown gypsy skin
they leave silver trails behind.
You try to brush it away
thinking it's bits of spider silk.
But it's deeper. You can't wipe it off.
Your skin will soak it up, your blood will keep it.

Arno Peters has rediscovered the world.
On his map
Africa is a large ochre-ripe papaya.
America lurks
in detergent green shadows.
I know I've made the mistake
of loving America too much.

Afterwards she wanted to eat tomatoes and raw onions.
Then numbers made too much noise

around her forehead,
and if she closed her eyes she could see the insides
of books she'd read.

Chew on pine-needles and look at the moon.
Then you'll know what to do.
If you taste the difference between
topology and topography it'll make all the difference.

When I say *witch* I can't have you thinking of Medea
or Macbeth or Salem.
I can't have you thinking at all.
After she swallowed the bone marrow
she could control
the blood in her brain.
If she wanted a silent nothing
she could make it in her brain.

What is magic? What is freedom?
His favourite leather jacket, gentle grey,
that he gave her, has power. When she smells it
she finds the words she needs. Slowly the jacket
is beginning to smell of her,
so when he wears it again
he'll smell of her and he'll know exactly
what to do, exactly where to go.

Sometimes if you get lost in America you'll see freedom:
Silver threads hanging from trees,
wet silver around that horse's mouth.

He told her to put the 'h' back
in *Ostertorsteinweg*. So she did.
She does so everyday: Magic *Osterthorsteinweg*
on clean envelopes.

If the tomato is *rot*
then I'll always imagine rotten tomatoes.
Although *rot* isn't pronounced like rot.
Although *rot* can be red as red bursting ripe fat red

as spurting red as ready to be cut up and cooked
immediately red. That's *rot*.

When he discovered she was a witch it was easier.
Then she could feel at home with him.
And as for him, well, he was looking
for a witch who would speak to him.
She was surprised.

When she brings Iowa April maple leaves indoors
her brain refuses to sleep,
her bone marrow makes different blood.
Then all night she hears *Osterthorsteinweg* and Hölderlin.
All night she understands the parts of Hölderlin
that I don't understand.

I've fallen through the cracks of vocabulary lists.
Below all grammar rules. And then what?
Can there be anything without grammar?
Well, there are tomatoes growing everywhere.
My fingers smell of their leaves.

When the witch spoke to him, when she touched his hands
he got some magic,
he got what he was looking for.
Although she had no intention
of giving him any. It just happened.
For a while she was cautious, uncertain.
Then she let him
have all the magic he needed.

Where is the common ground?
Arno Peters decided to trim Europe down
into pink bits.

I'm trying to figure out how the waters stay apart.

What does it mean to feel at home?
Sometimes when you walk into a house
and wander through the rooms until you feel the doors

and windows snug around you,
when you walk across the wooden floors and feel
blood clots in your throat then you know
it's the wrong house.

What if it's the wrong country?

He knew how to make pictures with her magic.
And so it was good.
When she had to leave *Osterthorsteinweg*
her magic wanted to turn into a lioness.
When she had to leave her magic became
distraught and out of focus so he gave her
his leather jacket.
The next day when she woke up she was
in the wrong bed, she was in the wrong country.
It took her 5 minutes to figure it out
with reason and logic. But there's no
freedom in logic. No logic to freedom.
No magic in logic.

How can she feel at home in so many places?
How do gypsies know when to leave?

If you brew tea in the strong teapot
with the good force in your fingers
and the long thoughts in your head during
the silver season then. . . .

They taught the 4-year-old girl to pick tea leaves.
They needed tender young fingers to break off
the most delicate leaves. They taught
the 4-year-old girl to massage the legs
of 80-year-old men and tired
pregnant women. They needed tender young
fingers to ease out the burning muscles.
Afterwards they fed her the young goat's
fresh marrow.

Once while backpacking up the Appalachian trail
somewhere in Massachusetts I met freedom.
She was tall, 5′ 10″ and had long white hair.
She said she was almost 60.
It was the end of August.
She'd been on the trail since Georgia
and was headed for Maine. She was alone.
I thought she was a dream. But I can show you
how she moved,
how she bent her head when she combed her hair.

That's why Arno Peters had to change the map.
That's why I took the word *witch*.

There are magic coins in the leather jacket.
Something burns whenever she touches them.
If she buys anything with those coins she'll lose
the power. She wears a turquoise blouse to cool her blood.
She wears silk to cool her magic, her logic....